Don dug out his penlight and followed the tunnel to the right. It seemed to go down, down, down, until he felt as if he were in the very center of the earth. Suddenly a door stood in his way. He shone the light along the edges, looking for some way to open it. He saw that the door was slightly raised at the bottom. At a touch it rose higher.

He took a tentative step into thick black silence. He swallowed nervously. He was soaked in icy sweat. He played the light over the stone floor . . . and shrieked.

Mummies, skeletons, bones, and skulls lay in scattered piles! He tried to swallow, but couldn't. His breath came in harsh, raspy gulps. The penlight dropped from his slippery fingers.

The light went out. Total blackness.

He started to back out when he heard a thud behind him. The heavy door had fallen into place.

He was sealed in the chamber of death!

TERROR IN THE TOMB OF DEATH

by *Alida E. Young*

cover illustration by Richard Kriegler

For Donovan, a very special grandson.

Thanks to my son, Ben, for taking me to Egypt so I could write about the country. And to my brother, John Quick, for giving me a computer so I could write the story.

Thanks also to some of my writer friends who have been so helpful and supportive over the years— Milly, Peggy, Bea, Bob, Donna, Madge, Elsie, Ruth, Charlene, and Ree.

Published by Worthington Press
7099 Huntley Road, Worthington, Ohio 43085

Copyright ©1988 by Worthington Press

Printed in the United States of America

10 9 8 7 6 5 4 3 2 1

ISBN 0-87406-321-3

One

DON'S eyes caught the headlines in a Cairo daily newspaper: THE MUMMY'S CURSE AFFAIR. His parents' pictures were plastered all over the front page. He bought the English-language paper from the airport newsstand and caught a taxi to the Red Tulip Hotel.

Mummy's curse? A ripple of fear made his hands go damp. The paper shook slightly as he quickly read the story.

> *Two months ago, the Hunts, an American archaeological team, discovered the tomb of an unknown prince. The mummy was in an outer chamber. It is expected that when the inner chamber is uncovered, the tomb will hold treasure far richer than King Tut's.*

5

On the mummy case are the words

WHOEVER TOUCHES ME OR MY TREASURE WILL BE CURSED FOR ETERNITY.

An icy chill ran down Don's back. A curse? Nobody believed in curses these days. He had no reason to be worried about his parents. He wadded up the paper and shook his head, trying to get rid of dumb thoughts of curses.

At the hotel, Mohammed, who was at least as old as the pyramids, shuffled out to the taxi and grabbed the bags. He was wearing a ragged, tipsy turban and a traditional *galabia*, a kind of long, striped cotton nightgown. He gave Don a cheery "Hel-lo-ooo," and grinned widely, flashing his one gold tooth.

"As-salaamu aleikum," Don greeted the old man, using his best pronunciation.

"Wa aleikun assalaam!" Mohammed replied.

"Hi, Mo! How's it going?" Don asked.

"Hel-lo-ooo."

"I just heard that a tornado knocked over the pyramids, and Martians are coming up the Nile," Don added.

"Hel-lo-ooo."

It was plain that Mohammed's English had not improved since Don's visit last summer.

Don followed the old man to the open

elevator to go to the lobby on the fourth floor. For some reason, you could take the elevator to the fourth floor, but no higher, and never down.

The elevator creaked and groaned its way up. It banged alarmingly, but Mohammed's golden smile said *Don't worry.*

Don stepped into the Tulip lobby. It always reminded him of an old movie. The lobby's sluggish ceiling fan hardly stirred the stagnant air or disturbed the lazy, fat flies.

Mohammed set the bags by the desk and gave Don a beaming smile.

Don's parents had been coming to the Tulip for years. They preferred it to the large tourist hotels. At the Tulip, everybody made you feel like one of the family.

Miss Hassani, the desk clerk, gave Don a warm greeting. "Ah, Mr. Donovan Rutherford Hunt, welcome to the Red Tulip again. It's nice to have you here for another summer."

Only his mother and Miss Hassani ever called Don by his full name. Miss Hassani was wearing a jacket with the Tulip emblem on the pocket. Last year Don had thought the Red Tulip was a dumb name for the hotel until he'd learned that tulips originally came from the Middle East, not Holland.

Miss Hassani helped Don put through a call

to his grandparents back in New York. He'd barely hung up when Ali, the bellboy, came running in from the back room. He was dressed exactly like his grandfather Mohammed, except he wasn't wearing a turban. Ali was 16, a year older than Don. He gave Don a hug and kissed him on both cheeks in the traditional greeting between friends. It always made Don feel a little weird to have a guy kiss him. He grabbed Ali's hand and shook it. "It's great to see you again, Ali."

"Hi, Dono, old buddy, old pal, old chum. Give me five."

Ali spoke with a British accent, and the American slang sounded funny.

Don grinned and hit Ali's palm. "Where did you learn English? From old comic books and TV?"

Ali grinned back. "And how many Arabic words have you learned since last summer?"

Ali not only spoke English and Arabic, but he knew a little German and French. He was just about the smartest kid Don knew.

They each took a bag and started up the narrow, dark staircase. On every landing was a bare bulb that couldn't have been brighter than 60 watts.

"Have you read the paper yet?" Ali asked.

"Yeah," Don said. "They're making a big

deal out of the mummy's curse bit. If the president of Egypt gets a cold, the papers will say it was caused by a 3,000-year-old virus."

"Don't joke about it, Dono. It's serious."

"Oh, come on. Nobody believes in curses."

"Maybe not, but a fire burned part of the barge that carried the mummy to Cairo. And a rock fell on a worker near the tomb. It nearly killed the guy."

"Accidents happen. And the fire was probably started from a charcoal stove near some papers."

They came to room 603. In the dim light, Ali's face looked pale, and his voice was low. "Don't make fun of things you don't know anything about."

"I'm sorry, Ali, but I grew up on spells and curses. On my fifth birthday I got a plastic, take-apart skeleton and a witch doctor's mask. I can't get excited over a mummy's curse." But as he said the words, another chill swept over him, and he shivered. "This hall is colder than a tomb."

"You wouldn't understand about curses. You're not Egyptian." Then Ali poked Don's arm and said in a lighter tone, "But now that I think about it, you sure look like one of those old statues in the museum."

Amazingly, Ali was right. Don didn't look

Arabic like Ali. Ali's skin was dark, and his eyes were black. And Ali was thin with narrow hips. Don was taller and a little lighter-skinned. He had elongated, green eyes, high cheekbones, and a hawklike nose. He looked just like pictures of the pharoahs.

Ali unlocked the door to room 603, and they went in. The room was clean but bare. The only furniture was a bed, an old chair with a broken spring, and a small, round table.

"We're saving 604 across the hall for your parents," Ali said. "They'll be here tomorrow."

Ali hung the garment bag on a hook. Don opened the other bag, then took out a box, and handed it to Ali.

Ali just stood there shaking and squeezing the box.

"Go ahead and open it," Don said.

Ali lifted off the lid and took out a pair of American jeans and athletic shoes. "Man, oh, man," he cried. "They're just like yours." He sat on the floor, kicked off his sandals, and tried on the shoes. "They fit perfectly, Dono."

"They'd better. It's a long way back to New York to exchange them."

"The shoes are great. The jeans are great. I'll look just like a tourist!"

Don grinned, happy that Ali liked the gifts. "I'm beat from the trip. I think I'll rest a while.

But let's do something later. Okay?"

"You bet. We can practice karate. But right now I have to get back to work." Ali clutched the gifts to his chest. "Thanks, Dono. *Alf shukran!* These are super-great."

After Ali left, Don stretched out on the hard bed. The pillow felt as if it were filled with sand, and he pushed it aside.

He thought about Ali. It was a funny thing about Ali and him. Don's parents were archaeologists. And his grandfather Hunt was an expert on American Indians. But it was Ali who dreamed of lost civilizations.

Don sighed, wishing he knew what he wanted to do with his life. He supposed he'd become an archaeologist, but so much of the work was painstaking and grubby. He'd rather be training for a marathon. But unfortunately, there weren't many jobs for runners.

As he was drifting off to sleep, he thought about the newspaper story. Ali was pretty uptight about the mummy's curse. Don hoped his parents were being extra careful . . . .

* * * * *

Don awakened drenched with sweat. He glanced at his watch and was surprised to see that he'd slept four hours. At least now there'd be water for a shower. The water only came on from seven at night to seven in the morning. Even when it did come on, it was hardly ever warm. And it was usually rusty, with a peculiar musty odor.

Don saw towels, soap, bottled water, and a plate of fruit and nuts. *Ali must have brought the things while I was asleep,* he thought. *I'd have slept through anything—even a hippo using the bed for a trampoline.*

Don ate some fruit and took a shower. There was water, but it was cold. And he had company in the bathroom. There were two enormous cockroaches, nearly the size of mice, under the sink.

When he came out of the bathroom, he noticed a piece of paper on the floor by his room door. It was a note written in Arabic. Ali was probably getting even with him for the crack about his English. But one word, printed in English in bloodred letters, jumped off the paper: HELP!

Maybe it wasn't from Ali, after all. Don hurriedly dressed and ran down to the lobby. He found Ali watching television.

"Ali, did you write this note?"

Ali looked at the paper. "Not me."

"Well, somebody slipped it under my door. Will you translate it for me?"

They went to the desk where Ali could see better. "It says, 'I have important information about your parents. Come to the spice bazaar in Old City.' It's signed 'Gemini.' "

"Do you think it's some kind of trick?" Don asked.

"I don't know. How would anyone know which room you were in? Maybe it was meant for your parents."

"Maybe so. I think I'll go over to the museum. If this has anything to do with Mom and Dad, the Director of Antiquities might know about it. Want to come with me?"

"Nope. I have to watch the desk for Miss Hassani."

* * * * *

Outside, the evening air was balmy. Don was always surprised that Cairo, being so close to the desert, was humid.

The museum was only a few blocks from the hotel. Don found a guard who spoke English. He told the guard his parents' name and asked to speak to the Director of Antiquities. In minutes he was led to the section of the museum that was being set up for the expected treasures from the tomb his parents had discovered.

Don loved the old museum. It had been built in the 1880s. It was dusty and dark, and you could hardly read the identification cards on the exhibits. But the place made him feel as if he'd stepped back in time. He'd spent so many hours here that he probably knew more about Egyptian history than most Egyptians.

Don saw a blue light coming from an adjoining room. Crossing to the door, he peered in. The room was bare, except for a mummy standing upright in its open wooden case. The coffin was decorated with gold and turquoise. The blue light gave the place a spooky look. Don stood by the door for a minute, staring at the mummy.

Something seemed to draw him closer to the mummy. Don leaned forward to get a better look at the medallion lying on a table near the coffin. A bird resembling a hawk or an eagle was etched on one side. On the other side was the Eye of Horus, one of the Egyptian gods.

Don knew better than to touch the artifact, but some strange force seemed to pull his hand to the medallion. An uneasiness filled him. His breath caught in his throat. The medallion felt—warm! He jerked back his hand. The uneasiness turned to fear as he bent over to read the identification card that was written in both hieroglyphics and in English.

WHOEVER TOUCHES ME OR MY TREASURE WILL BE CURSED FOR ETERNITY.

Don had scoffed at the idea of a curse, but now in this bare room, under the eerie blue light, it was a lot easier to believe.

His mouth turned dry. His breath sounded harsh, and his knees turned rubbery.

Suddenly, a movement caught his eye. He stiffened and slowly looked up. Had the mummy actually moved? Had a piece of the linen wrapping slipped from around the mummy's eyes? Don swallowed hard and tried to laugh. It was just his imagination. Of course it was. A mummy dead for thousands of years couldn't move.

But now the finger that had touched the medallion burned . . . and throbbed. Could there have been poison on the medallion? Ice ants crawled along his neck, and although the room was warm, Don shivered uncontrollably.

The mummy's arm slowly rose. A scream bubbled to Don's throat. He looked around wildly. "It's moving!" he cried. "It's alive!"

Don was alone. There was just the mummy and him.

He wanted to run, but he felt the strange force again. It was coming from the mummy—

or from the medallion. He wasn't sure, but there was something evil, something horrible about the mummy. He shuddered with fear. Cold sweat soaked his shirt.

Suddenly, terror overcame the power that was holding him there, and he slowly pulled himself away. Then he tore out of the museum and ran past the startled guard into the street. Heart pounding, he raced toward the hotel.

After a few blocks, he slowed to a walk. He felt as if someone were watching him.

This is dumb, he thought. *The mummy couldn't have moved.* Ali would kid him about acting like a jerk, but he couldn't get rid of the fear.

Now that he was walking slower and his breathing wasn't so loud, he could hear his own footsteps in the silent street. Oddly, there weren't many people around. He couldn't ever remember Cairo so quiet. The palm trees cast strange shadows, and the streetlights looked like pale, dead moons.

Don heard a padding sound behind him. *Sliiiip-thud, sliiiip-thud,* like someone or some thing dragging one foot. For a second he froze. Then he felt a burning at the back of his neck, and he began to run again.

Sliiiip-thud, sliiiip-thud, faster and faster behind him.

Two

DON raced into the hotel, shouting, "Mohammed! Mohammed!"

The old man was nowhere in sight. The elevator was locked. Gripping the railing, Don climbed up the dark stairwell to the fourth floor. His heart was hammering against his chest, and his breath rasped in his throat. The lobby was empty. A strange, sweetish odor filled the air, but there was no sign of life. He banged on the desk bell.

Where was everybody? He felt as if he were in a nightmare where he was alone in an alien world. He moved cautiously to the window. Keeping out of sight, he looked down on the street. Lurking near the entrance was a dark figure—or was it only the shadow of a palm?

Don took a deep, quivering breath. He must be imagining things. It was crazy to think that a mummy could walk out of a museum—even

17

crazier to think a mummy could walk at all. *In the morning, I'll feel pretty silly about this,* he thought.

He raced up the stairs to his room and locked the door. Without turning on a light, he looked out the window. The moon shone brightly on the alley below. The alley was empty. Nothing but shadows. He breathed a deep sigh. "Donovan Rutherford Hunt, you're a jerk," he told himself.

Even though the room was hot and stuffy, he closed the wooden, lattice-work shutters. Totally wiped out now, he slumped on the bed. Moonlight filtered through the lattices, turning the room a sulfurous yellow. Just as he started to relax, he heard a *snick-snick* of metal against metal. He quietly got to his feet and crouched, waiting.

The key turned in the lock. He pressed against the far wall and shivered. Then slowly—agonizingly slowly—the door opened, and he saw it.

THE MUMMY!

The linen wrappings had come loose from its arm, and it was motioning him forward. A sweetish, sickening odor filled the room.

Don gave a shaky laugh. "Okay, Ali, I know it's you. Where'd you get the Halloween costume?"

Growling deep in its chest, the figure moved toward him.

"That's a great act, but I know it's you, Ali. Real mummies can't walk." Don poked the mummy in the chest.

"Aaaaaaaagggggghhrrr!"

Don stumbled back, only now realizing that the creature was taller than either Ali or himself.

"Aaaaaaaagggggghhrrr!"

Don wheeled around and rushed into the bathroom. He locked the door, but knew it wouldn't hold for long.

The window. He glanced out. He was seven stories from the ground—too far to jump. Then he noticed a rickety old fire escape outside the window. It was really just a rusty metal ladder attached to the wall. He hoped it was sturdy enough to hold him.

The doorknob rattled. He needed more time. Frantically, he looked around. He grabbed a bottle of shampoo and poured it on the floor next to the door.

The knob rattled again, then slowly twisted.

Don yanked down the plastic shower curtain from the rod and stood to one side of the door. The smell of mildew on the plastic made him nauseous. He could hardly control his shaking hands.

The mummy crashed against the flimsy door, splintering it. *"Aaagh!"* it roared. It broke through and skidded on the slippery floor.

Don waited long enough to throw the curtain over the mummy's head, then he ran to the window and squeezed through.

For a moment Don was stuck. He wriggled furiously. A hand gripped his ankle. He wanted to scream, but the yell was frozen in his throat. He kicked out as hard as he could.

"Aaagh!" the mummy groaned.

Don grabbed the metal rung of the fire escape, pulled himself out, then scrambled down. But before he reached the ground, the metal stairs broke loose from the building, and he fell the rest of the way, crashing into a pile of boxes and trash.

Stunned for a minute, he shook his head. He was afraid to move for fear the mummy might find him. He stayed hidden until he felt safe enough to go look for Ali.

Keeping in the shadows of the building, he edged his way to the entrance of the hotel. He saw no one. He crept silently up the stairs to the lobby. It was still empty. Where was the night clerk? Where was anybody? He had to find Ali.

Don raced up the stairs to the top floor,

then climbed the ladder to the roof. Laundry flapped in the breeze. As he crossed to Ali's shack, chickens in pens along the wall started squawking. "Ali?" he called softly. "It's Don."

Ali poked his head out of the opening. "Dono? What are you doing up here?"

"I—I'm scared." He tried to keep his voice from shaking. "I know you're going to think I'm crazy, but—"

"Come over by the wall," Ali whispered. "Grandfather needs his rest."

Don grabbed Ali's arm. "The mummy followed me from the museum!"

"What?"

"I'm not kidding. The mummy was in my room."

"You just had a bad dream, Dono. Go back to sleep."

"I wasn't dreaming, and I'm not nuts. I'm telling you, a mummy was in my room." Don's voice rose. "It stunk, and it made noises. It might even still be there."

Ali sighed. "So how did this mummy get into your room? Did you lock your door?"

"I'm sure I did. Could it have gotten the key from the desk? Mustapha, the night clerk, wasn't there when I came in, and he's not there now."

"That's some smart mummy." Ali frowned

21

and searched Don's face. "You really did see a mummy?"

Don nodded and shivered. "I don't want to believe it either. But I saw it. It touched me." Don shuddered.

Ali hesitated a second, then said, "Come on. Let's see why Mustapha isn't at the desk."

They hurried down to the lobby. It was still empty.

Ali went behind the desk. He waved to Don. "Dono! Here."

Don looked over the high desk to see the night clerk on the floor. Mustapha was just coming to and holding his head.

Ali questioned him in Arabic.

"What'd he say?" Don asked excitedly. "Did he see the mummy?"

"He says he was dozing and didn't hear anyone come into the lobby. Somebody hit him on the head, but he didn't see who did it."

"Maybe we'd better call the police," Don said.

"Who'd ever believe a crazy story about a mummy running around the Tulip Hotel?"

"What about Mustapha's hit on the head?"

"He could have dozed off and fallen—okay, I believe you that something weird's going on. But the police won't help us."

"Look, Ali, let's check my room. If the

22

thing's not there, let's go to the museum. That mummy is important to my mom and dad."

"We'll look in your room, but I'm not going to the museum with you."

"Okay, okay, but let's get upstairs," Don said.

They climbed the stairs to the sixth floor. In the corridor outside his room, Don noticed a wet trail on the wooden floor. "Look! That proves it. The mummy came this way!"

"Come on, Dono, the maid probably spilled some tea."

Don tried the door. It slowly opened. The two of them stood there, eyes wide. Don's heart beat furiously. He swallowed hard and stepped inside.

Ali gasped at the sight of the broken bathroom door, the soapy shower curtain, and the wet floor.

"Now do you believe me?" Don whispered.

"I believe that something attacked you. But I still have a hard time believing a 3,000-year-old mummy can walk around Cairo."

Don went out into the corridor and followed the wet trail.

"Ali, come and look," he called. "The wet marks stop right in front of the ladder to the roof. I'm going after him."

They hurried up to the roof, but there was

no sign of a mummy. Ali checked his grandfather, who was snoring loudly. "He's okay," Ali said.

Don looked around. "It had to have come up here, Ali. Where could it have gone?"

The two stood at the edge of the roof, looking over at the next building. "Do you think it could have jumped across?" Don asked.

"That's a five-foot leap. But I guess if it can break down a door, it can jump across to the next building."

"I'm going to the museum," Don said. "It'd go back there, wouldn't it? Please come too, so I can prove I'm not nuts. The wrappings ought to be wet."

"No way, pal. It's scary there at night."

"How do you know?" Don asked.

"The father of a friend of mine used to work there," Ali said. "When we were little, we'd sneak into the museum through the air vents, then pretend we were pharaohs."

"Let's go then."

"I haven't been there at night for ages. Those vents may be sealed off now."

"Why did you stop going?" Don asked.

Ali gave a sheepish laugh. "One time when the museum used to open the mummy room to the public, we got trapped in there all night. I had nightmares for years about being locked

24

in there with those mummies.

"Come on, Ali, I just want to make sure the mummy's back where it ought to be."

* * * * *

When they got to the museum, a black Mercedes parked nearby caught Don's attention. A pair of large, fuzzy white dice were hanging from the rearview mirror. The dice looked weird in the big, expensive car.

Don followed Ali over a fence at the back of the building. "From now on," Ali whispered, "don't talk. We don't know where the guards are."

On hands and knees, they crawled through the vents. Swirls of dust filled Don's nose, and he stifled a sneeze. At the opening to the main floor, near some large statues, Ali came to an abrupt stop. "Ssh!" Ali hissed. "There's someone in there."

Quietly, Don moved up close to Ali and looked over his shoulder. He expected to see cleaning people. Instead, two men in dark coveralls and stocking masks were setting dynamite. Realizing that the mummy was in the next room, Don whispered, "You get the police. I'll try to scare them off."

Ali nodded, backed up, and squeezed past

Don. "Be careful," Ali said.

Don watched the two men for a minute. Where were the guards? Shouldn't there have been some kind of alarm? Don's mind whirled, trying to come up with a plan. But fate took over. He sneezed loudly.

For a second the men froze, then they took off.

Don had started to back through the vent when he noticed the sticks of dynamite. His father had taught him all about explosives, especially dynamite. He saw a flame inching its way along a fuse toward the explosive.

Don't go off!

As Don pushed back the vent cover and scrambled out, his pant leg caught on a piece of metal. Frantically, he tried to break free.

The flame was halfway to the dynamite now.

With a tremendous jerk, he broke free, tearing a gash in his leg in the process.

Don't go off! Please don't go off yet!

Ignoring the pain in his leg, he scrambled to his feet, rushed across the room, pulled the blasting cap and fuse free of the dynamite, then stamped out the flame.

He sank against a life-sized statue of the Pharaoh Tuthmosis. His breath came in great gasps. His heart hammered so loudly he thought someone would hear it. *The explosion could have destroyed priceless treasures—maybe even the mummy in the next room. And I could have been blown up,* he thought.

Still trembling, he moved slowly to the eerie blue light, not sure whether he hoped the mummy was in its case or gone from the museum. He peered inside.

The mummy was in its case. Beside it was a pedestal that hadn't been there earlier. The blue light gleamed on a portrait mask of gold and turquoise. Don stared at the mask of the young prince, and an eerie chill ran down his spine. The face looked familiar—green eyes and a hawklike nose. He swallowed the huge lump in his throat. A person could sure get some strange ideas in a museum at night.

Fidgeting with nervousness, Don wished Ali would hurry back with the police. They'd never catch those two men now. Don started to crawl back through the air vent, but something seemed to draw him toward the table where the medallion lay. He began to feel a pressure in his ears, as if something were tugging at his mind, forcing him toward the medallion.

Don's hands grew damp, and he felt tomb-cold. Sweat trickled down his neck. An invisible force drew him closer and closer to the mummy. A foul stench was in the air. Against his will, he picked up the medallion, turned it over, and stared into the Sacred Eye of the god Horus.

The room began to spin. Still holding the medallion, he threw out his arms to catch himself. But he felt as if he were falling, falling, whirling into a black void. The terrible pressure in his head grew worse. A hot wind swirled around him like the whipping of many wings, beating, beating, smothering . . . .

Three

THE whirling stopped, and Don found himself in a strange place. He slowly became aware of heat, searing heat, on his face. He squinted in the glare of the sun on the stark limestone cliffs. Crawling out of the shimmery white heat, he made his way along a narrow ledge.

Below him he heard the soft murmur of voices, and he stopped to listen.

"I tell you, Cobra, your twin must die. Falcon is eldest by an hour. It is he who will take your father's place as ruler of Upper and Lower Egypt."

Don carefully moved closer so he could see the men. One was dressed in a long, white, pleated skirt. Around his neck hung a wide gold collar decorated with turquoise. It was the vizier, the counselor to the king and the most powerful man in Egypt, except for the Pharaoh.

The other was a young man wearing a white pleated skirt and sandals. When the younger one turned around, his face looked familiar.

For a few minutes Don listened to the men discuss the death of Falcon, then he crept back along the ledge.

"Dono!" The voice sounded far away.

"Dono, wake up!"

Startled and disoriented, Don looked around wildly. He was in the museum. The mummy was safely in its place. *What a dream!* Don glanced at his watch. Only a few minutes had passed. "Ali, am I ever glad to see you! Wow, I just had the weirdest dream."

"Tell me later," Ali said. "We have to get out before the police swarm in here. I made an anonymous phone call."

"What about the museum guards?"

"I think they were drugged." Ali sounded anxious. "Come on. I don't want to have to explain why we're here."

"Did you see the men leave?" Don asked.

"Yeah. They jumped into that black Mercedes we saw."

Don's hand burned, and he looked at it, only then realizing he was still holding the medallion. As if the medallion were on fire, he dropped it onto the table. "Let's get out of here," he said.

At the door, Don looked back at the mummy. Could he have somehow been dreaming about the mummy's life? The voices he'd heard had used the name *Falcon*—could the bird on the medallion be a falcon? And what about that strange force that had seemed to draw him into the Eye of Horus?

"Come on, Dono," Ali whispered.

Hurriedly, they made their way back through the vent and off the museum grounds. They didn't stop running until they were safely back in Don's room at the hotel.

Don sank onto the bed. Ali slumped into the rickety chair.

Ali blew out his breath in a whistle. "What's going on around here? First, you think you see a mummy—"

"Think! I know I saw it. It was here."

"Was the mummy in the museum wet from the soapy shower curtain?" Ali asked.

"I don't know. I was too busy putting out the fuse to the dynamite. I didn't get a chance to check. Why do you think those men wanted to blow up the place?" Don asked. "Were they trying to destroy the mummy?"

"Could be," Ali said. "Some fanatical groups don't want Americans to get all the glory."

"That doesn't make sense. Why would they

want to destroy a priceless treasure? Anyway," Don said, "I'm glad we got there in time."

"What were you doing when I got back?" Ali asked. "You looked like you were in a trance."

Don shook his head. "I don't know. I guess I was dreaming, but it was the weirdest dream I've ever had. And it seemed so real."

"I don't know how anyone can fall asleep standing up," Ali said. "And your eyes were open. I still say you were in a trance or something."

"Maybe I was," Don said slowly. "There's an eye on the back of the mummy's medallion. I was looking into it, and suddenly everything went dark. I felt as if I were falling into a black hole. Then suddenly I was on a ledge in the sun. I was on one of the limestone cliffs like in the Valley of the Kings. It was hotter than blazes."

"I think you got too much sun in that dream."

Don ignored Ali's smart remark. He told Ali about the vizier saying that Falcon must die.

"How'd you know the guy was a vizier?" Ali asked.

Don thought for a moment. "I just knew, that's all. But the weirdest part of it is—you're not going to believe this—but the young guy named Cobra looked exactly like the portrait mask of the mummy in the museum."

"That makes sense. You were staring at the mask when you looked like you were in a trance. Anyway, you always did have a great imagination."

"You won't believe this either," Don said. "I'm starved."

"Did you ever eat dinner?"

"Come to think of it, no."

"I'll get you something." Ali stood up and stretched. "I'll get the maid to clean up the mess in the bathroom, too."

While Ali went down to the kitchen in the basement, Don turned on his radio to an English-language station to see if there was any news about the break-in at the museum.

The eleven o'clock news came on.

"More about the so-called Mummy's Curse Affair. Tonight, the police found evidence of a plot to destroy the mummy that was recently discovered by a team of American archaeologists . . . ."

When the short newsbreak was over, Don switched off the radio. Were his parents in danger? He hadn't heard from them since a few weeks ago, when they'd called him on his birthday. Usually they made it home for his birthday, but this year they'd been at the tombsite and hadn't wanted to leave. They were so close to reaching the treasure.

Treasure . . . the word always made him think of his fifth birthday. His mom and dad had taken him and five of his friends to a restaurant. They'd eaten hamburgers and fancy desserts, and had all been given prizes and balloons and noisemakers. A clown had even performed tricks.

On the way home, it had started to rain, and the air was damp and cold. Don's dad had lit a fire in the fireplace, and the three of them had sat on the floor in a circle, holding hands.

That night they'd told him he was adopted.

"Oh, Don-Don," his mother had said, and hugged him. "We could find Egyptian tombs filled with gold and jewels, or find an eight-foot, solid-gold Buddha in Thailand, or discover the lost continent of Atlantis, but we will never find a treasure more precious than you."

Don hadn't really understood what *adopted* meant. All he knew was how much they loved him, how special they made him feel.

Ali's knock broke into Don's thoughts. Ali had brought a tray with lamb and rice, a pot of black tea, and the crusty rolls Don loved.

They didn't even talk while they were eating. When they finished, Ali said he was going to bed. "I don't care if 10 mummies are running around the hotel, don't wake me up."

Don nodded and said good night, but he was thinking about the prince in his dream and the medallion's strange power. Tomorrow he would go to the library or the university. He wanted to see if he could find out anything about some twin princes named Falcon and Cobra. The portrait mask had looked so familiar. *Maybe I've seen a picture of one of them somewhere,* he thought.

He closed his eyes, trying to remember the mask. Green eyes . . . hawklike nose . . . . Then it hit him. He looked in the mirror. No wonder the mask had seemed familiar. It looked like him!

Four

B Y the time Don awakened the next morning, the hotel had already turned off the water, and he had to brush his teeth with bottled water. While he was dressing, he noticed the note telling him to come to Old City. What kind of information could someone give him? And why the word *HELP*—in red? Maybe it was just a new gimmick for selling something, but after everything that had happened the day before, he had to find out what the note was all about.

On the way out, he asked the desk clerk to tell Ali he was taking the bus to Old City.

Don headed for the bus station, then changed his mind. The buses were always jammed and had people hanging on to the outside. Then there were always people hanging on to the people hanging on to the bus. He decided to walk.

As he headed for Old City, he tried to figure out what the note could mean. The word *HELP* written in red worried him. And who was Gemini? Too many things had been happening lately. Feeling uneasy, Don kept looking over his shoulder.

He passed mud-brick houses and ancient mosques, high-rise apartments, and the garlic market with its pungent odors. The air was rank with diesel fumes and greasy smoke. The streets teemed with people, honking cars and buses, and herds of camels marked with red on their way to slaughter.

Men of all ages swarmed about, pulling, jostling, begging him to buy tourist items. They had plaster models of the Sphinx and scarab charms, guaranteed to have come from King Tut's tomb. When Don had first come to Egypt, the haggling had bothered him, until he realized that selling fake artifacts was the only way some people could earn enough to eat.

In the bazaar he walked past metal workers, hammering and beating copper and tin, and stalls selling everything from plastic sandals to rolls of silk.

At one stall an old man was selling blue, pink, and green glassware made from broken bottles and sharp pieces of mirror. A sign in English caught Don's eye.

HOROSCOPES.
THIS IS YOUR LUCKY DAY.

Don caught the old man staring at him. "American?" he asked Don.

Don nodded. *Horoscopes,* he thought. *Gemini. It's a zodiac sign.* "Are you Gemini?" he asked the old man.

The strange man shook his head and held out a horoscope etched on the back of a green glass scarab. "You take," he said.

Don refused to take the glass beetle.

The man crooked his finger, beckoning Don to come closer. "This is your lucky day. I sell very, very cheap. Scarab come from tomb of newly discovered Prince Falcon. For you, cheap."

As he talked, he stared into Don's eyes. The man's black pupils grew larger and larger, then he backed away. "You are not American. You are—" He thrust the green glass beetle into Don's hand. "Take it. You are in great danger!" He looked quickly up at the sky. "Danger from the past!"

The hair rose on Don's neck and arms. "What are you talking about? How do you know—"

"Go! Leave Egypt!" The man whirled around and disappeared into the crowd.

Danger from the past? Weird, really weird.

Don shoved the scarab into his pocket and was headed for the spice bazaar, when a ragged young boy sidled up to Don and whispered, "Gemini say for you to go see the Zabalin."

"Wait!" Don cried, and tried to catch the boy's arm. But just as the old man had done, the boy disappeared into the crowd.

Don felt a chill of fear. Maybe he should just head back to the hotel. But if this Gemini had any information about his parents, he had to find the Zabalin. *Zabalin? Zabalin?* Then he remembered they were the garbage collectors of Cairo. Was this a trap?

There was only one way to find out. Instead of walking, he took a taxi to the huge garbage dump where thousands of Zabalin lived. As he paid for the taxi, the driver looked at Don suspiciously.

Don hurried away from the taxi. As he walked along the dirt track past goats and donkeys and piles of rotting garbage, he tried to hold his breath. The stink was awful, and the flies were worse. How did people live in these tiny buildings made of boxes and rusty tin right in the midst of huge piles of garbage?

A donkey-drawn cart passed, towing the hulk of a wrecked car.

When no one stopped him, he began to

think the whole thing was a hoax. He was about to head back to town when he saw a man on a bicycle jouncing along the rutted pathway.

When the bicycle got close, the man jumped off. Don took a karate stance.

"It's all right," the man whispered. "I'm Gemini. Follow me."

Don hesitated, again wondering if he was stepping into a trap. He wished he had brought Ali along. He'd been stupid to come out here all alone. But his curiosity was stronger than his need for caution.

He followed the man past stacks of rags piled higher than the shack where a woman and three children were sorting through the garbage. They were salvaging scraps of cloth and plastic. The children smiled at Don. The woman was singing as happily as if she were in a palace instead of a garbage dump.

Don sat on an old tire, while Gemini squatted in the doorway of the shack.

"Okay," Don said, trying to keep his voice from showing fear. "I want to know who you are. You leave a stupid note under my door and go through all this spy stuff. Who needs help? Is it my parents? What's going on?"

"Please calm yourself," the man said. "For the time being it's best you know me only as

Gemini. It's the code word we use for anything to do with the young prince Falcon and his tomb. I work with your parents."

"How do I know that?"

"Your father is six feet four, and weighs 210 pounds. He has a scar on his left shoulder, and in private he calls your mother Baby Doll. And he likes the New York Mets. Your mother is five feet four, with reddish blond hair and hazel eyes. Her favorite foods are Boston clam chowder and fried prawns. When your father is upset he cracks his knuckles, which makes your mother say, 'Craig Hunt, you're driving me crazy!' and he will say, 'Shari, honey, it's a putt!' "

Don grinned and nodded. "Yeah, you know them, all right. So how come you didn't come to my room and knock and cut all this superspy jazz?"

"I was afraid of being followed. I had a boy leave the message under your door. The Tulip has no phones in the rooms. I could not call you. The same boy delivered the message in the bazaar so I could see if you were being followed."

Feeling very uneasy, Don looked around quickly. "Was I?"

"I'm not sure. But please, I haven't much time."

Don looked at his watch. "Me, neither. Mom and Dad will be here tonight." He could hardly wait to see them.

Gemini looked away. "I—uh—I wish I didn't have to tell you, but . . ." He hesitated.

Don jumped up. "What's wrong?" He grabbed Gemini's arm. "Are they all right?"

"They have disappeared. Yesterday, I went into Luxor for supplies. When I returned to the tombsite, they were gone. All the workers had disappeared. I couldn't find any of them at their homes. Something has frightened them away."

"I'm going to Luxor!"

"No. You must leave Egypt. Now."

Don stared at Gemini. "There was a bomb scare at the museum last night. Is there a connection?"

Gemini shrugged his shoulders. "I'm not sure. It seems that someone doesn't want us to excavate the tomb."

A terrible thought struck Don. "Do you think Mom and Dad were kidnapped?"

Gemini shrugged again. "It's possible. We can only wait to see if someone asks for ransom."

"I'm not leaving Egypt." Don said firmly. He tried to make his voice sound more confident than he really felt. If anything had happened

43

to his mom and dad . . . .

"I don't want to frighten you more than necessary, Don, but in case the worst happens, there's something else I have to tell you."

"Nothing's going to happen!" Don shouted. "You have to help me!"

"I've notified the authorities, but we want to keep it out of the press. You must leave," Gemini said, his voice sounding urgent. "If your parents were kidnapped—you could be next."

"I'll be careful. But what did you want to tell me?"

"We haven't much time." Gemini looked quickly around. "I don't dare stay anyplace too long, so just listen and don't ask questions until I finish."

Don nodded.

"A few months ago my Zabalin friend who lives here found a box buried under an old aqueduct. It looked ancient, and it contained a scroll. Knowing I'm an expert in ancient languages, he gave me the box. I worked with your parents in Iran and Syria, so I passed the box on to them.

"The scroll was written in Thebes by a young prince who called himself Falcon. He claimed he was the real heir to the throne, and that Cobra, his twin, had tried to kill him, then switched their name medallions."

Don's mind flashed to the dream he'd had in the museum. A chill ran down his spine. In the dream, Cobra and a vizier were planning to kill Falcon.

"That's why we used the code name *Gemini*. The symbol for the zodiac sign Gemini is the twins."

"Are you saying the mummy in the museum isn't Falcon, the heir, but the twin, Cobra?" Don asked.

"If the writer is telling the truth, that's the case. Also, in the box was a funerary urn containing the heart of Prince Cobra. As you undoubtedly know, the ancients believed that the soul resided in the heart. The scroll led us to the tomb. We found the mummy in an outer chamber, as if someone had tried to move it."

"Where are the scroll and urn now?" Don asked, his mind spinning with questions.

"In the hotel safe."

"The Red Tulip hotel safe? Isn't that a dumb place?"

"Sometimes the most obvious is the safest. And besides, only your parents, you, and I know about the twins. There is no record of them in history." Gemini got to his feet. "I have to go, Don. We shouldn't be seen together."

"But how can I find you?"

"In—"

Gunfire cut off his words. Don dove for cover. Bullets thudded into piles of boxes and struck the metal of the shack, almost deafening him.

Five

TIRES screeched. A black Mercedes spun around. More bullets sprayed along the ground—a nice neat line. Dust spurted up in Don's face.

"Run!" Gemini cried. And as if to lure the car away from Don, Gemini took off, running deeper into the garbage dump.

Keeping low, Don darted from one mound of trash to another, until he was out in the streets. He stumbled on, constantly looking behind him, expecting bullets to whiz past his ears. His chest hurt, and he gasped for breath, but he kept on running.

He headed toward the Cairo cemeteries, thinking no one would follow him there. The cemetery was like a real city for the living, with streets and stone houses. He leaned against a huge, fancy tomb so he could catch his breath. As he gulped in air, he heard the sound of a powerful engine.

The black Mercedes! The men had followed him!

Don ran, but he stumbled and fell. The car door opened, and a man yanked him into the backseat. He tried to use his karate moves, but he was too exhausted. Kicking and flailing his arms, he screamed. A hand clamped over his mouth. He tried to bite the man's fingers and struggled to get loose. Just as he recognized one of the men who had set the dynamite in the museum, a black hood came down over Don's face.

Gemini was right, he thought. *They want me, too. Are they just trying to scare me—or are they going to kill me?*

As the car took off again, Don stayed silent, trying to memorize all the turns. But after what must have been hours of driving, he lost track. Finally, the car slowed almost to a stop. The door opened with a rush of air. He felt a sharp push, then he was falling. He hit the dirt with a thud and rolled as far from the wheels of the car as he could.

A staccato blast ripped the air. Expecting to feel bullets tearing into his body, he yanked off the hood in time to see the Mercedes roar off in a cloud of dust. He was almost hysterical with relief when he realized the "shots" had only been backfire from the car. For a few minutes he sat there stunned from the fall. But except for aches and bruises, he wasn't seriously hurt.

After a while, he struggled to his feet and looked around. He had no idea where he was or which direction to take to the city. The stars were just coming out. He had never studied astronomy, but even if he had, he wondered if the stars would look the same in New York and Egypt.

Yet, as he stared up at the heavens, the formation of the stars and planets seemed familiar. Somehow, he knew that to reach the Nile, he must keep the North Star to his right.

As he took off at a run, his mind whirled with questions. Was Gemini dead? Where were his parents? Why hadn't the men gagged him and bound his hands—or killed him? But most important, what did the information about the twins Falcon and Cobra mean? The only thing he knew for sure was that he had to get help— and fast.

Each step was agony. The moon was like a white skull in the dark sky, showing him the way to Cairo.

Don was weaving with exhaustion when he reached the hotel. He had no idea what time it was, but thought it must be near dawn.

Mohammed was not at his post, and the elevator was locked. Don slowly climbed the four flights to the lobby to tell Ali what had happened. With every step he wondered if the men would be waiting.

Gemini had told him to leave Egypt, but how could he? How could he go without knowing what had happened to his mom and dad?

The lobby was empty. No Ali. No desk clerk. Thinking maybe Ali was taking a guest to a room, Don sat in the alcove to wait. He was thinking about the twin princes, Falcon and Cobra, when he heard the elevator start up.

The *locked elevator* was coming up.

Second floor.

Third floor. He heard it bump.

Mohammed had the only key. Who was in that elevator? It clanged. Stopped. The metal door rasped open. Then he heard it.

Sliiiip-thud, sliiiip-thud, across the tile floor. *Sliiiip-thud.*

Don stood rooted, unable to move, his heart pounding rapidly.

The mummy limped into the lobby. The linen wrappings had come loose, and Don could see evil green eyes and smell dank mold. It was wearing the Falcon medallion.

Sweat soaked Don's shirt. He wanted to run, but his feet wouldn't move. An overpowering force seemed to hold him.

He looked around for a weapon.

Nothing.

Then he saw the bottled water on the desk.

The mummy limped toward him. Don's breath caught in his throat. He tried to scream, but the only sound that came from his paralyzed throat was a whistling gasp.

Desperate now, Don grabbed the bottle of water and threw it.

Glass shattered. Water spewed over the mummy's chest. The mummy staggered back, and the medallion glowed with a poisonous green light that reflected in the mummy's eyes.

Nothing seemed to stop it. It limped closer. And closer. Don could feel its breath. Its shriveled black fingers closed about Don's wrist and clamped tight. It smelled of death.

Don struggled, but the creature had the strength of a demon.

The mummy picked him up as if he were a baby. Shuddering, half sick from the smell, Don tried to make himself dead weight.

The mummy relaxed its hold for a second. With all his strength, Don struggled loose and ran, stumbling down the stairs to the street.

He heard the screech of tires, felt the impact.

Jagged, orange-red pain. Darkness . . . .

Six

DON awakened slowly to find himself on a straw mat. He tried to remember what had happened.

The mummy! Don sat up quickly. His head felt as if it would explode. Then he remembered running from the mummy and stumbling down the stairs and into the street. He checked his body. He was bruised and scraped and sore, but nothing seemed to be broken.

The only light came from a wavering candle flame. Wax puddled on the stone floor. Don didn't recognize the windowless room. It smelled musty and—what was that?

He heard a hissing sound and swung around to see a cobra crawling out of a basket by the door. Don froze, almost hypnotized, too scared to move or yell. The snake slithered a foot or so across the stone floor. Its forked tongue flicked in and out, sensing the heat of a body.

It crawled closer and closer to the straw mat.

The cobra raised the front part of its body and flattened its neck, preparing to attack. It swayed from side to side.

Don sat still as death, his heart pounding.

"Don't move," a voice whispered.

Out of the corner of his eye, he saw Ali slowly, very slowly, get up off a mat on the other side of the room. Ali picked up a short-handled broom, and just as the snake struck out, he hit it. Then carrying it on the wooden handle, he put it back in the basket and slammed down the lid. "Don't worry about him," Ali said. "I've taken care of plenty of snakes before."

Don let out a strangled sigh. "Ali, this just hasn't been my day!"

"What happened, Dono? I heard the screech of tires and someone scream. Then I found you at the edge of the street, muttering about machine guns and mummies and twin princes."

"You'd never believe what all has happened. But how'd I get here? Where are we?"

"In the basement. I was afraid to take you to your room, so I brought you down here to the storeroom." He looked toward the basket with the snake. "Somebody put that in the room while we were asleep. We'd better find a safer place."

"I don't think there is a safe place," Don said.

Don told Ali all the things that had happened since he left for the bazaar in Old City. He dug into his pocket for the scarab. "Some guy shoved this at me and said I was in danger from the past." Don threw the scarab across the room.

Ali looked at him as if he were crazy. "Are you sure you didn't get a bump on the head when you collided with that car?"

"I told you that you'd never believe me. Sometimes I think I'm going nuts," Don said ruefully. "But you saw the men at the museum, the Mercedes, and the note from Gemini."

"I can buy all that, Dono, but a mummy coming up in the locked elevator? Come on. You had to be dreaming."

"That mummy was as real as you are," Don said. "But there's something strange about it."

Ali gave a little laugh. "The whole thing's strange, if you ask me."

"Ali, let's go upstairs. I want you to open the safe for me. Gemini told me about a box my parents put in the safe. Maybe I can find something in it that will make sense."

Ali was shaking his head. "I don't know

about that. I could get into trouble."

Don just stared at him for a minute. "Think about it. How can we get into worse trouble? I feel as if a pyramid fell on top of me. I've been shot at and left in the desert to rot. And now somebody's let a cobra loose where we were sleeping. That's not exactly a friendly gesture. I'd say we're in big trouble already." Then more seriously, he said, "Maybe there's something in the box that'll tell me what's happened to Mom and Dad."

"All right. But just remember, this is your idea."

They went up to the office, waited for the desk clerk to leave for a minute, then Ali opened the safe. Don carefully lifted out the ancient metal box.

"I don't think you should go back to your old room." Ali took down a key to a different room. "We never use this room unless we're completely full."

Checking to be sure no one else was around, they hurried up the stairs. Ali unlocked the door to the new room, and they quickly slipped inside. The small, windowless cubicle had enough space for only a narrow cot and a table.

Don looked around. "No wonder you don't rent this often. The cockroaches in Egypt are bigger than this room."

Don set the box on the round table and raised the lid. "I'm glad it wasn't locked. I'd have had to pry it open."

Ali came over to the table to look inside. "Wow, look at that. An ancient funerary urn."

"Gemini said it contains the heart of one of the princes. I think I'll take his word for it." Don started to lift out the papyrus scroll.

"Be careful, Dono. That may be a priceless artifact."

"I won't touch it. I sure can't read ancient Egyptian." But under the scroll, he saw another scroll that looked far newer. "Hey, look at this, Ali."

"Maybe you shouldn't touch that, either," Ali said nervously. "Your parents might not want you to look at it."

"I have to do anything I can to find them." Don took out the scroll and unrolled it enough to see that it was written in English. "This might tell us where the tombsite is."

"But you said your mom and dad aren't there now."

"I know, but there might be some clues here."

He unrolled the scroll farther. "Anyway, it has my name on it."

Don read the words aloud. *"To Donovan—*
when he is old enough to understand."

The rest, he read to himself.

Dear Donovan,

Perhaps we should have told you this
when we explained that you were adopted,
but we decided to wait until you were
older.

We found you in a cave near the Valley
of the Kings. You were almost dead
from exposure and hunger.

We loved you from the moment we saw
you. We were so afraid the authorities
wouldn't let us take you, but after much
haggling, we were allowed to adopt you
and bring you back to the States.

We knew that someday you might want
to track down your real parents, but there
was no trace, no clue to whom you might
belong. All we know is that we love you
dearly.

With all our love,

Mom and Dad

Tears welled up in Don's eyes. "Oh, Ali, what
if I never see them again?"

"They're too famous to just disappear," Ali
said, but not very confidently.

Don told Ali what the scroll had said. Instead of shock at the news he was Egyptian,

Don felt a sense of rightness. "No wonder I've always felt I belonged here," he said with awe. Then he poked Ali on the shoulder. "Who knows? We might be related."

Ali shook his head. "I have Arab blood. It's obvious you're descended from the Ancients."

Don thought about how much he looked like the funeral mask of the prince. Maybe the mummy had been trying to tell him something. But then he remembered the hate in those glittering green eyes.

"Ali, I have to go to the museum to check the mummy. I broke a bottle of water over it. Maybe the linen wrappings are still wet."

"So you were the guy who made the mess in the lobby. Mustapha had a fit."

"Will you come to Luxor with me?" Don asked. "We can take the first train after I go to the museum. Dad'll pay you just like before."

Last year, Mohammed had let Ali act as Don's guide. At the Red Tulip, Ali worked 12 hours every day and made about 26¢ a day, plus room and meals—if you could call the shack on the roof a room.

"I'll go see if Mustapha can spare me for a couple of days," Ali said. "You'd better get some sleep. It's almost morning. And it's a long ride to Luxor."

Don nodded. "Thanks, Ali, for everything—

mostly for not thinking I'm completely nuts."

Ali grinned. "Who says I don't? I'm going along as your keeper," he said, and ducked out of the room.

Don reread the scroll. As he was putting it back, something shiny underneath the ancient scroll caught his eye. He carefully lifted out a small, metal box and opened it. Inside was a medallion exactly like the one the mummy had been wearing, except that a cobra was etched on it.

Almost afraid to touch it, he picked it up and turned it over. On the other side was the Eye of Horus. It felt warm to his fingers. Once again, he felt the strange magnetic power. He couldn't look away from the eye.

The air seemed to churn and writhe around him. Don felt a pressure around his head. The world was black now, and he was being sucked into a whirlpool, spinning through time and space . . . .

Suddenly, Don could see Falcon in a palace. Falcon and Cobra were fighting.

Cobra turned away. His face was ugly, like some devil beast. A dagger with a jeweled handle gleamed in Cobra's hand.

"Oh, the great Falcon, the twin who is so swift of foot. The twin who is so wise. The twin who hides his true face. You may fool others, but not

me—nor the vizier. We know that you would not rule Egypt as our father did. You would empty the palace coffers to feed the poor. You would not levy the proper taxes, and soon there would be no mighty land by the Nile."

"The gods made air and water for every man," Falcon said.

"The vizier is right about you. Before long Egypt would grow weak." Cobra raised his arm.

Falcon snatched up a piece of cloth and wound it around his hand. As he circled slowly, he watched Cobra's eyes, waiting for the attack.

Cobra charged.

Falcon deflected the blow with his bound fist, and at the same time, kicked upward. The dagger clattered to the floor. They both dove for it. Cobra grabbed it and stabbed Falcon in the chest.

Cobra dragged his brother from the room and threw him over the back of a donkey. When they were far into the desert, Cobra switched the medallions, then left Falcon to die in the searing heat.

Falcon slowly regained consciousness. His wound was not deep. Dazed from pain and exhaustion, burned by the relentless sun, his feet bleeding, Falcon limped back to the city. There he learned that his brother had been poisoned. Cobra had been wearing the Falcon *medallion. No doubt the vizier had thought he was killing Falcon.*

"Dono! Dono! What's the matter with you?"

Don looked up, startled. "I—I was dreaming, I guess." He shook his head, trying to throw off the strange visions.

"I came back to see if you wanted to put the box in the safe before Mustapha or Miss Hassani realizes it's missing," Ali said.

"I guess I should."

Ali frowned and pointed to Don's hand. "What's that you're holding?"

"I found this medallion in the box. It's just like the one at the museum, except it has a cobra on it. Ali, whenever I look into the Eye of Horus, I can see what happened in the past—or else I'm dreaming. I'm not sure which. Cobra tried to kill Falcon and left him in the desert to die. Falcon was trying to get to the city to stop the vizier from becoming Pharaoh."

Ali shook his head slowly. "I'm getting worried about you, Dono. Strange things happen in Egypt, but this scares even me. Maybe we should tell somebody."

"Who?" Don asked. "I don't know who to trust. And anyway, who'd believe us?"

As Don closed the box, he kept the medallion, hiding it in his hand. He wanted it with him to see if he could discover the secret of its power.

"Tell Miss Hassani I'll need some of the money Dad always leaves for me in the safe," Don said. "I'll see you as soon as I get back from the museum."

"Try not to worry, Dono. I'll keep watch in the halls."

This time Don didn't argue. "Thanks, Ali. You're a real friend."

* * * * *

The next morning, Don packed a few things in his flight bag, placed the medallion in his pocket, and headed for the museum, keeping his eyes open for any sign of a black Mercedes.

In the bright sunlight, he began to doubt that the mummy had come to the hotel. It had to be some kind of fake to scare him away. Sure—Ali was right. Three-thousand-year-old mummies didn't just walk around the streets of Cairo. He almost had himself convinced to go on over to the train station and buy the tickets to Luxor. But he just had to find out about the mummy. In spite of his fear, he climbed the steps to the museum.

Mr. Kahlil, an assistant to the Director,

knew Don by sight, and took him to the room where the mummy was being prepared for viewing by the public.

"Did Mr. and Mrs. Hunt return to Cairo?" Mr. Kahlil asked.

Not sure who he could trust, Don kept silent about his parents' disappearance. "They were delayed," Don said. "Do you have any idea who set the bomb here?"

"There are always fanatics," Mr. Kahlil said. "We doubled the guards."

Don stopped in the doorway to the room, a sudden fear sending his pulse racing. "It would sure be awful if something happened to the mummy," Don said. "Is it okay if I get a closer look?"

"I see no harm," the man said with a smile. "After all, it was your parents who discovered Prince Falcon."

"Do you know anything about him?" Don asked, trying to sound as casual as possible. "Did he have any brothers or sisters? How did he die?"

"There are no records of him. We are hoping the excavation of the tomb will tell us more about our mysterious prince."

His heart in his throat, Don moved closer to the mummy case. *This is stupid*, Don thought. *What do I hope to see? Even if the wrappings had been wet from the bottled water, they'd be dry by now.*

Mr. Kahlil turned on the blue light. Something glistened on the wrappings. Don leaned closer. He stifled a gasp. The hair rose on his arms and neck.

A fragment of clear glass!

Seven

THE sleeper train to Luxor in Upper Egypt swayed from side to side. For the first time since he got off the plane in Cairo, Don could relax a little.

As he sat next to the window, watching the sunset reflecting on the Nile River, he saw the country with new eyes. This was the land of his ancestors. Boats with triangular sails were silhouetted against the backdrop of the palm trees that edged the water. Along the dirt paths, men in white *galabias* were riding on donkeys and camels laden with palm fronds or sugar cane. *Am I related to one of those men?* he wondered. A sense of belonging filled him.

"Are you hungry, Dono?" Ali asked, holding out the basket of food he'd brought along.

Don took a piece of round bread, some chick-pea balls, and grapes, but he left the onion. Ali ate his onion as if it were an apple.

When they finished the meal, Don pulled out the medallion, being careful to touch only the chain.

Ali stared at the medallion with suspicion. "You should have left that in the safe, Dono."

"I wanted to see if it affected you the way it does me." Don held it out to Ali.

Ali shrank back.

"It won't bite you. Just hold it and look into the Eye of Horus."

Gingerly, Ali took the medallion and stared at the eye.

"Does it feel hot?" Don asked.

"Nope. Actually, it's cold. I don't see anything or feel anything."

Don took it back. "That's weird. For me, it's almost like looking into a crystal ball."

"You've always been alone when you looked into it before. Do it while I'm with you, and tell me what you see."

"Okay, I'll try," Don said.

"Maybe it's like being hypnotized," Ali said. "I'll ask questions. If you can hear me, answer."

They were both a little afraid of what might happen, but Don held the medallion, rubbing it gently with his fingers. He looked into the Eye of Horus.

The air seemed to grow thicker, heavier,

threatening. A funnel of wind seemed to suck him into its center. Don gasped for breath.

"Dono, stop! Drop it!"

Faintly, he heard Ali calling him as he seemed to float through space . . . .

Falcon hurried to the temple. Sixty-nine days before, the priests had begun preparing Cobra's body for the long journey through eternity, his body preserved so that his spirit could return to it at will.

"Dono! Don, can you hear me?"

Ali's voice sounded hollow to Don, as if it were coming through a long tunnel. "Yes," he whispered.

"Where are you?"

"Falcon's in a temple. He's dressed in peasant's clothes so no one will recognize him."

"What's he doing?" Ali asked.

"You don't want to hear this."

"Tell me, Dono."

Don took a deep breath. "I'm watching the priests clean out Cobra's body. They're filling it with aromatic spices. They placed something that looks like the lungs into a small urn with a stopper lid carved like a baboon. The liver is going into an urn with a stopper carved like a human head. The heart is going into one with a scarab stopper.

"The priests are washing his body and wrapping it in a whole lot of linen. One is reciting, 'You will live again forever.'

"Ali, somehow I know what Falcon is feeling, even what he's thinking. *Brother, some day we will meet again, and I will tell you the truth about your death.*

"Falcon's going to the tomb now. It's close to his father's. I've never seen anything like it. The old pharaoh's tomb is much larger, and it's filled with treasure. It's been sealed off so grave robbers can't find it.

"The vizier is overseeing everything. It's plain he's the most powerful man in Egypt. Everybody's treating him as if he's already the new pharaoh. Falcon's angry because he knows the guy poisoned Cobra."

"Can't Falcon do anything about it?" Ali asked.

"He doesn't dare let anyone recognize him or the vizier would have him killed, too.

"Ali, I don't believe this. The vizier's stealing the urn with the heart. Falcon's following him to a building where the priests store urns. The vizier's hiding the urn with the heart among all the empty ones. Without his heart, Cobra can't return to his body in the next world.

"The old guy's left now. Falcon is getting

the urn. He's taking it to an old hut where he and Cobra used to play. He's putting the urn in a copper box. Ali! It's just like the one in the hotel safe—only it's new and shiny.

"Ali, I'm so tired . . . ."

"Come back, Dono. Now!"

Don heard the rumble of wheels on metal and felt himself swaying from side to side in rhythm with the rumble. Slowly he opened his eyes to find Ali leaning over him, his face furrowed with worry.

"Are you all right?" Ali asked.

"I'm fine. Just tired. Ali, could you hear what I was saying, or was I just dreaming it?"

"I heard."

Don grabbed Ali's arm. "Ali, I knew what Falcon was thinking and feeling. I want to try it again and find out what happened to him."

"No, Dono! Somehow, you're too close to him. If something happens to him—you might—I don't even want to think about—"

The train jerked to a stop, wheels screeching, cutting off Ali's words. They were both thrown out of their seats. Don scrambled to his feet and looked out the window, but it was too dark to see anything.

"It must be some kind of emergency," Ali said.

Don started to turn from the window when

71

he saw a light. The light from the brakeman's lantern shone on—the black Mercedes!

"Ali! We have to get out of here! Those men have tracked me down. They're getting on at the back."

Ali started gathering their things. "Leave them! There's no time!" Don said. Stuffing the medallion in his pocket, he rushed out into the corridor and hurried to the front of the train.

They passed through the hot, smelly, third-class car that was crowded with people and boxes and animals. As passengers looked up, startled, Ali said something in Arabic, and touched his lips with his finger.

A whistle blew, and the train began to move again, picking up speed. The motion jerked them from side to side, battering their arms and shoulders.

A rubber, accordionlike tunnel connected the cars. As they hurried through it, Don could see the ground rushing by underfoot.

"Follow me," Ali said. "And pray!"

There was a slight opening where they could get through at the point where the accordion tunnel connected to the car. Ali squeezed through, making his way to the outside of the train.

No way am I following him, Don thought.

But through the dirty window looking into

the economy car, Don saw the three men. He had no choice but to follow Ali. With his heart in his throat, he inched his way to the outside, trying not to look at the open area beneath his feet. The noise of the train was deafening. Ali was holding on to a narrow metal bar that ran nearly the length of the car.

The rushing air took Don's breath away.

Don reached out for the metal bar, but his hand slipped, and he banged against the side of the train. He made another grab for the metal bar, and this time he held on. The strain on his arms and fingers was almost unbearable, but the thought of those men made him hold on just a little longer.

A movement above him made Don look up. A man was crouched low, walking along the top of the train. Ali had spotted the man, too.

Ali moved as close to Don as he could and shouted over the roar of wind and the clatter of wheels. "We have to get off before that guy sees us."

Don nodded, not knowing how much longer he could hang on anyway.

"There's a station a few miles ahead," Ali said. "The train has to slow down for it. When I yell go, jump as far away from the tracks as you can."

Hours seemed to pass before the train

began to slow. Don's arms ached, and his fingers felt numb.

"GO!" Ali yelled, and dropped from the side of the train.

Don's fingers were so locked on to the bar that it was seconds before he could let go. He jumped as far as he could. He hit the ground with a jolt that jarred his teeth and knocked the wind out of him. As he rolled away from the tracks, he felt the ground tremble from the passing train.

He saw Ali a few feet from him. They stayed down until the train was out of sight. Then Ali crawled over to him. "Come on. We'll hide in those palms until morning."

Slowly, keeping low to the ground, they made their way to a grove of palms. Don gave Ali a wry grin and repeated the old Greyhound Bus ad, "Next time, try the bus!" Then he turned serious. "I'm sorry I got you into this mess, Ali. As soon as we get to Luxor, I think you should go home."

Ali shook his head. "I've come this far. I'm not turning back now."

Don reached out and punched his friend on the shoulder. "Thanks," he said simply. Exhausted now, Don stretched out his aching body. He felt his pocket to make sure the medallion was safe.

The next thing he knew, Ali was shaking him.

"Wake up, Dono. Time to go."

The sky was pearly gray. A ghostly mist hung over the land along the river. Don shivered. When he tried to stand, he was stiff and sore. "Did you get any sleep, Ali?"

"I kept watch most of the night." He pointed to the south. "There's a farmer's hut. Maybe we can buy some food."

* * * * *

They not only got food, but the farmer agreed to take them into Luxor in his donkey cart. Just in case the men tracked them down, they hid under a load of date palm fronds.

After a long time on the road, Don muttered, "I could walk to Luxor faster than this donkey."

"Sure you could. And the first car that passed would be the black Mercedes."

"I know, I know, but I'm really worried about my mom and dad, Ali. What if—what if they're . . ." Don's voice trailed off.

"Don't even think about it, Dono. We'll find them."

Don touched his pocket and felt the outline of the medallion. Why couldn't it show him the present, not just the past?

The farmer left them at the edge of town. Don felt far too conspicuous in Western clothes, so he gave Ali money to buy a *galabia* and a turban.

"See if you can find something to darken my skin, too," Don told Ali. "I'll meet you at the Lotus Hotel."

The two separated, and Don made his way to the small hotel where his parents always stayed. The desk clerk recognized Don from his visit the year before and gave him a key to the room. "But we have not seen Mr. and Mrs. Hunt for over a week."

Don went upstairs. Room 402 was full of the usual gear—suitcases, books, maps, cameras. But something felt wrong. Smelled wrong.

A chill slowly spread down his neck, down his back. The hair raised up on his arms. That sweetish, sickening smell was familiar. Then he remembered—his hotel room at the Red Tulip.

The mummy!

Eight

DON rushed downstairs and waited for Ali in the alley next to the hotel. Sweat poured down his neck and back, soaking his shirt. He kept brushing away the flies that buzzed around his face.

Finally, he saw his friend. As Ali skulked close to the buildings, his eyes darted from side to side.

When Ali passed close by, Don hissed, "Psst! Back here."

Ali wheeled around. "Dono? Is that you?"

Don reached out and grabbed Ali's arm. "Get out of sight!" he whispered.

Ali ducked into the shade of the alley. "What's wrong? Did you see the men in the Mercedes?"

"We have worse trouble than those men," Don said. "The mummy followed me!"

Ali just stared at him for a second. "This is

no time for jokes, Dono."

"This is no joke. I know it sounds crazy, but that mummy's been in my mom and dad's room. The mummy had the same sickening, sweetish odor when it was in my room at the Tulip." He gripped Ali's arm. "I have to find Mom and Dad. Ali, I'm scared."

For once, Ali didn't try to tell Don that mummies don't walk, that mummies don't travel over 400 miles. Instead, he handed Don a bundle. "Change into these clothes. I couldn't find anything to darken your skin, though."

Don quickly pulled on the nightgownlike *galabia*. "I wish I'd borrowed one of your outfits and sandals in Cairo. I hope nobody notices my sneakers."

"Lucky I didn't wear mine," Ali said as he twisted white material around Don's head to make a turban. "Well, I guess you're okay as long as somebody doesn't look too closely."

"Come on," Don said. "We're going to the City of the Dead."

They took a boat across the Nile where they hired two donkeys and bought bedrolls and enough supplies for three days. The sun was directly overhead when they finally took off to find the tombsite. Avoiding the tourist areas and main roads, they circled around the limestone mountains that held the Valley of the Kings and the Valley of the Queens.

"Do you have any idea how to find the tombsite?" Ali asked.

Don looked all around him. As far as he could see there was nothing but limestone mountains and rocky desert soil. "No, not really," he finally answered. "But Dad mentioned once that it was beyond the tombs in an area where no one had excavated before."

"Even if we find the tomb, what then?"

"I don't know, but I have to try to find Mom and Dad. Maybe we'll discover a clue there."

They traveled through the heat of the day. By the time it was dark, Don's backside was sore from the jouncing donkey ride. And his eyes burned and watered from the glaring sun.

Tired and hungry, they camped in a wide crevice between some rocks. Don shivered in the chilly night air, but they didn't dare light a fire. Don was glad he was still wearing his shirt and jeans under the *galabia*.

In silence, they ate their cold meal, then opened their bedrolls. Don was asleep almost before his head touched the blanket.

"Wake up! Wake up!" Ali's cries brought Don out of a dream about Cobra and Falcon when they were little.

Don jumped up, fully awake. "What's the

matter, Ali? What's wrong?"

"One of us should have stood guard! The donkeys are gone!"

They checked the tethers and found them cut. Don looked at Ali. "Why? If someone took our donkeys and supplies, why didn't they kill us?"

"Because they don't need to," Ali said slowly. "They know we'll die out here without water. We'd better go back."

"No, I'm not giving up yet."

"We only have our bedrolls, a flashlight, and a few dates. That won't get us far, Dono."

"But we each have some water in our canteens. Ali, I have to go on. You go back to Cairo. Maybe Gemini will try to get in touch with me there."

Ali looked grim. "I think it's crazy, but I'm not letting you go on alone."

"Thanks," Don said. "You're a real friend."

When they were packed and ready to go, Ali looked around. "Which way?"

"To the west," Don answered without even thinking. At Ali's questioning look, he said, "It just feels right."

With the morning sun at their backs, they started walking, picking their way through the rocks, looking for any sign that men or animals had come this way. Overhead a hawk circled and soared. "There must be something living out here," Don said. "That hawk has to eat."

During the hottest part of the day, they looked for a cave or even a hole in the rocks, anything to get out of the burning sun. But there was no shade. In the afternoon their water gave out, but they kept on.

A hot wind blew sand in their faces. Don's mouth was so dry he could hardly swallow. His lips were cracked, his tongue swollen. He could no longer see clearly. He felt as if there was no moisture left in his body. Would he soon look like a mummy?

"Dono," Ali croaked, "we're lost. I can't go on."

Don knew Ali was right. The sun was going down, and they were no closer to finding his parents. Exhausted and near tears, he sank down on the hot sand.

"I—I'm sorry," Don said weakly. "We should have turned back."

Ali handed him a date. "This is the last of the food."

Don ate the fruit slowly. It helped the hunger pangs, but it only made him more thirsty. How long could a person live without water?

At sunset the mountains turned coral pink in the setting sun. One of the mountains was shaped like an enormous pink crocodile. It seemed to be watching over them. He and Ali were too exhausted to talk, and their lips were too cracked. Don reached and touched Ali's arm. *I never should have asked Ali to come along,* he thought. *We can't make it through another day.*

He closed his eyes, wondering if he'd see the dawn. Absently, he rubbed the medallion. There was no rush of wind, no swirling into a black abyss. He drifted into sleep and dreamed of Falcon . . . .

He was resting at an oasis under the shade of date palms and olive trees where there was pure, clear water. He would stay here where it was safe. If the vizier ever discovered he was still alive . . . . His eyes filled with angry tears— not for himself, but for his people. What would happen to Egypt under the vizier's oppressive rule?

He picked up his knife and the green stone he'd been working on. He began to carve it into the form of a scarab. When the next caravan passed, he would trade it for needed supplies.

At sunset he gazed at the limestone mountain. Slowly it turned into a pink crocodile. Its snout was like an arrow pointing to his father's and Cobra's tombs. He remembered how he and Cobra used to see shapes in the clouds.

It was too dark now to carve, so he played his flute. The melody made him think of Cobra. If only there was some way to make him understand.

As the full moon rose and turned the sands to silver, jackals howled, and lions prowled in the distance . . . .

In the early dawn, the eerie sound of a jackal awakened Don from his dream. The dream had seemed so real, but there was no oasis, no water, no trees. Yet he could almost feel the dampness in the air.

"Ali! Wake up!"

Furiously, Don began to dig where the pool in his dream had been.

Ali sat up and looked at him as if the sun had melted his brain. "Sometimes thirst makes people do strange things," Ali said.

"Help me! The sand feels damp right here."

With renewed strength, they both dug in the sand until they uncovered a small pool of water. "Ali! We're not going to die! We're not going to die."

Laughing and crying, they got on their stomachs to drink the gritty water.

"Not too much," Ali warned. "You'll make yourself sick."

Don dunked his head and let water dribble down his face and neck. He wished he could lie in the water and soak for a year, but they had to go on.

They filled their canteens and loaded up their gear. As they were ready to leave, Don realized he didn't have the medallion. Almost in a panic, he searched for it. Finally, he found it where he had dropped it in his sleep. Luckily, it hadn't been covered by the sand.

"Which way now?" Ali asked.

"Toward the mountain shaped like a crocodile."

"Where?" Ali looked around. "I don't see any crocodile."

"You have no imagination," Don told him.

"And you have too much."

They trudged on through the day. But as they walked away from the rising sun, the outline of the mountain changed, and Don wasn't sure which was the one shaped like a crocodile. He began to have doubts about the dream.

After several hours, they rested under an outcrop of rock. As Don crawled along the ledge, a piece of loose rock fell and appeared to drop into a hole of some kind.

Carefully, Don made his way along the ledge. He saw an opening, a cavern of some sort. "Ali!" His voice echoed hollowly. "Come here. I think we can get in out of the sun."

Ali crawled up behind him.

"Be careful," Ali said. "There might be snakes."

Don hesitated. Then, gathering up his courage to go into the black unknown, he dropped into the huge cavern. Ali followed. Suddenly a rush of sound, a black wave came at them. Don screamed, "Bats!" He beat the squealing creatures, flailing his arms to keep them away from his face.

As fast as the bats had rushed at them, they were gone. For a long time Don and Ali sat in the dark, cool silence. Later, when Ali had finally fallen asleep from exhaustion, Don got quietly to his feet and began to explore the cave. It seemed so familiar.

Whispers seemed to bounce off the walls. *Your brother must die, or Falcon will become King of all Egypt.*

The whispers faded. For a moment Don felt as if he'd been in the cave before. He closed his eyes and ran his fingers over the medallion. So many thoughts spun through his mind. *Am I somehow related to Falcon and Cobra?* he wondered. *Or did I read about them in some book? How could a mummy walk? I've been watching too many horror movies,* he thought.

As he rubbed the medallion, his fingers grew hot. He stared into the Eye of Horus. *The mourners shrieked and tore at their clothing. They sprinkled dust on their hands. The priests carried the mummified body to the open tomb. . . .*

"Ali, wake up!" Don cried. He scrambled out of the cavern and looked around for landmarks.

"What's wrong?" Ali came out of the cavern as if shot from a cannon. "What's wrong?"

"I think the tomb is somewhere close."

"More of your weird dreams?" Ali began. Then he stopped. "But then again, your dream found us water."

Don inched his way along the ledge with Ali right behind him. Hearing a faint sound, he turned to Ali and held his finger to his lips. They both strained to listen.

"It sounds like something is going on deep inside the mountain," Don said.

Excited now, they tried to scale the steep slope. On hands and knees, digging in with their fingers, they climbed. Suddenly the loose shale gave way under their feet.

Ali screamed as he slid and skidded back down the mountain. He came to a stop a foot or so below Don. For a moment they lay still, afraid to move.

Then Don braced himself, got a firm footing, and tried to grab Ali's outstretched arm. But their hands didn't touch.

Don took off his belt and handed Ali one end. "Here, hang on to this. My sneakers grip better than your sandals."

Slowly, they made their way to the top of the ridge. Don stood up and took a deep breath of relief. Below him he saw donkeys, a jeep, tents, and even a helicopter. "Ali! This is it. We've found them! Let's go."

Ali came up beside him. "Dono, we have to be careful. Maybe we should wait until dark."

"I have to find Mom and Dad," Don said, but he did agree to wait until nightfall.

When it was dark, they cautiously made their way down—sliding, slipping, tearing their clothing. They checked the tents, but no one was inside. The donkeys snorted, but otherwise all was silent.

"Let's see if we can find an opening," Don said. "There had to be a way to get into the tomb."

Since the camp was empty, Don risked getting out his flashlight. They walked along, playing the light over the rocky sides of the mountain. "Look," Ali whispered. "Shine your flashlight along this crevice." After a minute, he said, "Here it is."

Not sure what they'd find, Don took a deep breath, then went in first. A few feet inside was a deep hole, with stairs cut into the rock.

"Do you think it's safe?" Ali whispered.

"I don't know, but I'm going down."

Don shone the light down the hole. For a minute they both stood there, neither wanting to admit he was afraid. Finally, they made their way slowly down a flight of stone steps to a chamber.

Two tunnels led from the chamber. Both the chamber and the tunnels appeared to be raw and new.

"Maybe we should separate and each take a tunnel," Don said. "We can cover more ground that way."

"Okay. Let's meet back here," Ali said.

Ali took the flashlight. Don dug out his penlight and followed the tunnel to the right. It seemed to go down, down, down, until he felt as if he were in the very center of the earth. Suddenly a door stood in his way. He shone the light along the edges, looking for some way to open it. He saw that the door was slightly raised at the bottom. At a touch it rose higher.

He took a tentative step into thick black silence. He swallowed nervously. He was soaked in icy sweat. Don played the light over the stone floor . . . and shrieked.

Mummies, skeletons, bones, and skulls lay

in scattered piles! He tried to swallow, but couldn't. His breath came in harsh, raspy gulps. The penlight dropped from his slippery fingers.

The light went out. Total blackness.

He started to back out when he heard a thud behind him. The heavy door had fallen into place.

He was sealed in the chamber of death!

Nine

DON crouched near the door and shouted, "Ali! Help!"

The chamber echoed his cries. His ears pounded and it was hard to breathe. There was only a little air coming from the base of the door, so he lay on the ground. He stretched out his arm and swept his hand over the rock floor, trying to find the light. His fingers touched something. "Aagghh!" He shuddered. It was a snake!

He scrabbled at the door until he was exhausted. He had no idea how long he lay there. Then, over the sound of his labored breathing, he heard a noise on the other side of the door. "Help me! Please help . . ." he gasped.

Suddenly the door rose. A beam of light hurt his eyes, and he tried to turn his head away.

"I thought I'd never find you, Dono."

At the sound of Ali's voice, Don nearly collapsed with relief. He filled his lungs with huge gulps of air.

"Ssh!" Ali warned him. "I heard men in one of the tunnels on a deeper level. They mentioned your parents."

Don got out of the chamber as fast as he could.

"Where's your penlight?" Ali asked.

"I dropped it back in there, but you won't catch me going in that place again." Don shivered violently. "It was awful. Skeletons and mummies and snakes . . ." He didn't want to even think about it.

Don followed Ali to a lower tunnel that continued for a quarter of a mile or so, then abruptly took a sharp turn. Ali put his fingers to his lips, and they crept forward toward the sound of voices. Just ahead, in a large chamber lighted by a kerosene lantern, four men were talking. They were speaking some Middle Eastern language. Ali seemed to understand what they were saying, but Don caught only a few words. One was the name *Hunt*.

As they crouched there in the tunnel, a million questions went through Don's mind. Were they too late? Had the men killed his parents?

Don nearly went crazy before the men finally left. When the sound of their voices faded away, Don turned to Ali. "What were they talking about?" he asked. "What did they say about Mom and Dad?"

"Your mom and dad are alive, but the men plan to—I'm sorry Dono—they plan to kill your parents sometime tonight. They don't want anybody to know about this place. But right now, they're planning to seal this tunnel. It leads to their arsenal where they have weapons stored."

For a minute Don couldn't take it all in. Terrorists. Weapons. "How do they plan"—he swallowed hard—"to kill Mom and Dad?"

"They're going to put them in the chamber you were in—the one with all the bones and mummies. Then they'll blast the tunnel leading to the chamber. They think the authorities will believe it's an accident . . . or the Mummy's Curse. What are we going to do, Dono?"

"I don't know. Let's see what's inside the chamber where the men were," Don suggested.

They found the chamber empty except for a stone sarcophagus and a pile of rags. And that strange, sweet smell. Don looked more closely at the rags. "It's a mummy costume."

Don picked up the costume and sniffed it. "I

smelled this same odor in my parents' room in Luxor."

Ali gave a feeble laugh. "Didn't I tell you the mummy wasn't alive?"

Don shook his head. "I agree that the mummy who came up to my room was dressed in this outfit. It smelled just like this. But the mummy that picked me up in the lobby smelled like death. In a million years you'll never make me believe that mummy was a fake."

"Come on," Ali said. "We don't have time to argue. Let's find your mom and dad."

"Just a minute," Don said. "I have an idea."

Breathing through his mouth because of the strong smell, Don quickly slipped into the mummy costume. "How do I look?"

"Scary. But what are you going to do?"

"If we bump into one of the men, maybe they'll think I'm one of them."

"Good idea," Ali said, handing Don the flashlight. "Which way?"

"I don't know. I've never seen any of this in my dreams."

As they headed down one of the tunnels, Don asked if Ali had seen any signs of another chamber.

"No, just the one you were in."

"That's where they plan to take Mom and

Dad." Don's voice broke on the words. *If the men blocked the tunnel, there'd be two more skel—* He pushed away that horrible thought.

"We have to hurry!" Don said. "Come on!" He took off at a run. The light bobbed up and down, making eerie shadows on the stone walls. They went only a short way when they became lost in the maze of tunnels. "We should have followed the men," Don said, beginning to panic. "We're never going to find Mom and Dad in time."

Frantic now, they rushed through the tunnels. "Stop!" Ali hissed. "I hear something up ahead."

All Don could hear was his own heavy breathing and the pounding of his heart.

Don covered the light with his hand and held it straight down. It gave them barely enough light, but they didn't want anyone to see them. They moved forward slowly.

A kerosene lantern lit up the passageway ahead. A man was closing the stone door of a chamber. It thunked down heavily. Then the man picked up the lantern and headed down the tunnel away from Don and Ali.

As soon as the man was out of hearing range, Don whispered, "I'll bet that's where Mom and Dad are. Come on!"

They hurried over to the door. Don put his

ear against it, but could hear nothing from inside. "Mom? Dad?"

No answer.

"They have to be in there," Don said. "But they couldn't hear us through these thick walls."

They tried to open the door, but it didn't appear to work the same way as the one closing off the chamber of skeletons. After working at it for a while, Don was getting more and more worried. "Ali, you stay here and keep trying. I'm going to see if I can find the arsenal. Maybe there are some explosives we can use to open the door."

"Be careful," Ali said.

Don started to leave, then realized that if he took the flashlight Ali would be in the dark. "I hate to leave you without any light."

"Go! At least the men can't see me."

Don headed in the direction the man had taken. Now, the layout of the tomb seemed familiar. He looked around at the walls. It was almost as if he'd been here before. He easily made his way down, down into what must have been the very center of the mountain.

Suddenly the tunnel opened into an enormous chamber. He crawled forward to get a better look. A man was going through a box, pulling out sticks of dynamite.

Paintings like the ones he'd seen in the Valley of the Kings covered the walls of the tomb. There were no treasures, though. *Grave robbers must have looted the tomb years before,* he thought.

In the light of the man's kerosene lamp, he saw boxes and barrels and rifles and enough weapons to start a third world war. He let out a soft, "Wowwww."

The man whipped around. "Ahmed?" he questioned. Then he said something Don didn't understand.

Don stood up and moved into the dim light. He slowly raised his arm and pointed at the man. *This guy might not know English, but he'll understand a threatening tone,* Don thought. "You have desecrated my burial place," Don said in a low, threatening monotone.

"You not Ahmed!" the man said in broken English. Then he backed up with a look of terror on his face. "Who are—"

"You ignored my curse."

As the man dove for the exit, his foot knocked over the lantern. He ran out, yelling, "Ahmed! Ahmed!"

Don couldn't believe how easily he had fooled the man. He hurried forward to see if he could find some grenades. But then he noticed the lantern had touched off a fire in the straw packing. In seconds it was blazing. Don frantically looked around for something to put out the fire. But there was nothing. If the flames reached the explosives . . . .

The fire spread, burning straw and packing materials—closer and closer to the explosives. The smoke was choking Don. He had to get out of there. Fast.

Holding some of the mummy bandages over his mouth and nose, he quickly searched through the boxes until he found a box of grenades. He grabbed two of them and raced out of the chamber.

The three men came running toward him. Don saw the stunned looks on their faces. He'd forgotten he was wearing the mummy costume. As much as he hated the men, he couldn't let anyone die. "Get out!" he yelled. "The explosives are going to blow!"

Choking, coughing, his eyes tearing from the smoke, he raced back to where he'd left Ali.

"What's going on?" Ali wanted to know.

"The arsenal's on fire! Hold the flashlight while I pull the pins on these grenades."

He pulled the pins and threw the grenades against the lower part of the door. "Get back!" he yelled.

The grenades exploded, but when the smoke had died down and they checked the door, nothing had changed.

Don dug at the door until his fingers were bleeding.

"Come on," Ali said. "We'll never get this open in time. We have to get out!"

"You go. I'm not leaving!"

Don aimed the flashlight along the edges of the door. *Think. Think.* He had seen the man close the door. He ran his fingers along the edges again. He knew that most tomb doors were like huge plugs, but this one was different.

Now, there was a louder explosion. The whole mountain was going up!

"Mom! Dad!"

Ten

ANOTHER explosion ripped the air.

Don dug into his pocket for the medallion and stared into the Eye of Horus. Almost as if in a dream, he saw the workers hewing out the chamber, setting the huge door into place. He could see how to work the door. He reached for the levering mechanism.

Slowly, agonizingly slowly, the stone began to rise.

"Dad! Mom! It's me. Come on!"

When the door had risen high enough, Don's parents and Gemini ran out.

"Hurry!" Don said. "The whole mountain's going to explode!"

Don led the way out. Stumbling and gasping for breath, they raced through the tunnels and out of the mountains. They kept on running, putting distance between themselves and the mountain.

The earth trembled beneath them, and they threw themselves flat on the ground. "Cover your heads," Don's father shouted.

Don buried his face in his arms and covered his ears. Like a volcano, the mountain exploded with an awesome roar. Pressure pushed against his ears. Limestone rained around them.

Silence.

Don realized he'd been holding his breath. He let it out in a gasp and cautiously raised his head. His parents and Gemini were sitting up, staring at the destruction. Tears filled their eyes, and Don realized what a terrible, terrible loss this was for them. All their work was gone forever. The tombs, the treasures— all lost.

But all Don really cared about was that his parents were safe. He rushed to his mother's arms. "Mom! Dad! I thought I'd never see you again."

"Oh, Don-Don," his mother said, and hugged him tightly. Suddenly, he felt like a small boy again. Tears filled his eyes, and he didn't even care if anyone saw him crying.

"I thought we'd had it," his father said. "But how did you and Ali find us?"

Don glanced at Ali. How could he tell his parents about the medallion and the mummy?

They'd think he was crazy. "I knew the general direction of the tombsite. We were lucky, I guess."

"What are you doing in that outfit?" his mother asked.

"I found the mummy costume and scared the men away with it." Just then they heard the sound of helicopters. "The explosion must have been seen and heard in Luxor," Don's father said. "We're in for a lot of questioning."

The choppers landed, spewing sand. Men in Egyptian military uniforms jumped out even before the sand had settled.

Both Don and his parents were able to give the authorities descriptions of the terrorists.

They were all taken to Luxor for further questioning, then flown to Cairo, where they had to repeat everything. Don could hear the suspicion in the voices of the police.

He whispered to his father, "They think we somehow caused the explosion. And maybe I did. If I hadn't scared the man, he might not have kicked over the lantern."

"Don, you can't go through the rest of your life what-iffing. If you hadn't done what you did, your mom, Gemini, and I would be dead now."

After hours of questioning, they were free to go to the Red Tulip Hotel. But except for Ali, they were all told to leave the country within 24 hours.

Already, the newspapers were full of the story.

MUMMY'S CURSE DESTROYS TOMBS.
American archaeologists claim
terrorist arsenal exploded.

In the taxi, they were all tired. Don's father sighed. "Well, at least we have the mummy. Without it, nobody would believe we'd actually found those tombs."

"I hope the museum's guarding it properly," Don's mother said. "It's the only thing we have to show for years of work."

But at least his mom and dad were alive. He hadn't realized until he thought he'd lost them how much he really loved them.

* * * * *

That evening, Don had dinner with his parents in their room. Don had worried for hours whether he should tell his mom and dad about the mummy and the medallion.

"There's something I have to tell you," he said hesitantly. "It's about the mummy."

"What about it?" his father asked. "We checked on it this morning. It's safe."

"I—I know you're going to think I'm nuts,

but—well, that mummy came to the hotel. It picked me up like—"

"But, Don," his father broke in. "You told the police it was one of the terrorists dressed up in a mummy suit."

"I know. That guy did come into my room. I think he was just trying to scare me so I'd go home. But the real mummy, the one you discovered in the tomb, tried to carry me away."

He saw the look his parents exchanged. "I know it sounds crazy. Like Ali says, 'How can a 3,000-year-old mummy walk around?' "

He pulled the medallion out of his pocket. "Something really weird's been going on. There are two of these things. One is in the museum, and this one I took out of the box."

He saw the startled look on his parents' faces. "I found the scrolls and read the one addressed to me," he said. "I know I'm really Egyptian."

"I'm sorry you found out about it that way," his mother said. "We wanted to tell you at the proper time."

"It's okay. The scroll said I was to read it when I was ready. Believe me, I was ready!"

"But you shouldn't have taken the medallion out of the box," his father said. "We have to turn these things over to the Director of Antiquities before we leave tomorrow."

"But I needed it. I wouldn't have found you without it. There's a strange force connected with both medallions. When I rub them or look into the Eye of Horus, I feel as if I'm going through a time warp. I look into this eye, and I see things that happened a long time ago."

"Don, your imagination can play tricks on you in this country," his father said. "You've studied so much about Egypt, it's no wonder that you dream about it."

Don knew there was no point in arguing. Maybe it was self-hypnosis or dreaming about things he'd read. Maybe he'd imagined that the mummy had picked him up . . . maybe.

"You're probably right," he said, "but I feel like I know the twin named Falcon. I even look like the face on the portrait mask."

He saw the look that passed between his parents. "You saw the resemblance, too, didn't you?" he asked.

His mother reached out and took his hand. "Honey, there's something else we haven't told you. When we were adopting you, we learned that you had a twin brother, but there was no record of what had happened to him."

Don stared at them in shock. "I'm a twin? Just like Falcon and Cobra," he said slowly. The hair rose along his arms and neck. "Do you think I could be related to them?"

"We have no way of knowing," his father said.

"But I'll bet I'm descended from them some way," he said excitedly. "I'll bet that's why I feel like I know Falcon."

Don's mind was racing. "I want to tell Ali. He'll go nuts." At the door, he stopped. "Dad, could I keep the Falcon medallion? I could switch them and put the Cobra medallion in the museum and—"

"They aren't ours to keep," his father said. "You know better than to even ask."

"I'm sorry. I'll go put this one back in the safe."

Don went to find Ali. He and Mustapha were watching an old *I Love Lucy* show on TV.

"Can I talk to you alone?" Don asked.

"Sure. Come into the office."

Don followed Ali to the little room.

"Ali, you'll never guess in a million years what my mom and dad just told me." He didn't wait for Ali to answer. "I'm a twin! Would you believe it—I'm a twin just like Falcon and Cobra."

"So? Lots of people are twins. Do they know where your twin is?"

"No, there's not any record of him. But maybe I'll come back someday and try to track him down. Don't you think that's weird, though, that I'm a twin like Falcon?"

"Just because you think you're descended from royalty, don't get any ideas." Ali grinned. "I refuse to bow to you, Your Lowness."

"Seriously, Ali, I need a favor. I hate to ask after the mess I got you into, but will you help me one last time?"

"How can I say no to a guy I might never see again?" His voice was husky. "I'm really going to miss you, Dono."

"Me, too. But maybe you can come visit me in New York."

"Maybe. What's the favor?"

"Late tonight, after everybody's sleeping, I want you to open the safe for me, then go with me to the museum. There's something important I have to do."

Ali was shaking his head violently. "No way, Dono. Not on your life. After all that's happened, if we're caught in the museum, we'll go to jail."

"We can go back through the vents. I only need to be there for a couple of minutes. Please?"

"You're always trying to talk me into things."

Don knew his friend was coming around. "Just think how unexciting your life's going to be when I'm gone."

"I can stand a little less excitement for a while. But what's so important?"

"I'll tell you later. Meet me here about midnight. And bring the key to the safe."

After Ali left, Don got a flashlight and went down to the basement. The storeroom was unlocked, and he slipped inside. He played the light over the floor. In the corner where he'd thrown it was the green scarab, glittering like a small green sun. He held it under the light. Could it possibly be the one that Falcon had carved thousands of years ago? He shoved it in his pocket. *I'm getting weirder every day,* he thought, and hurried upstairs to his room.

* * * * *

Don had set his alarm for 11:45. When it went off, he dressed in dark clothes and hurried down to the lobby. Ali and Mustapha were sitting in the alcove. The radio was on, but they both looked as if they were asleep.

Don touched Ali's shoulder, and he woke up instantly. Quietly, they slipped into the office. Ali opened the safe, and Don took out the scroll and the funerary urn with the mummy's heart. Then the two of them hurried to the museum.

Out of breath, Ali gasped, "What are you

going to do with that stuff?"

"You'll see when we get there."

At the museum, they had to wait for a guard to pass by before they could slip into the vent. Again, they crawled through the dusty tunnel to the mummy room.

"You wait here," Don said. "If you hear anybody coming, warn me and get out."

Don pushed the vent cover open and climbed out. He crossed to the mummy, and with shaking hands placed the urn with Cobra's heart at the mummy's feet.

He took the medallion out of his pocket and held it in his hand. With the medallion, he had no trouble understanding the ancient writing. In a voice husky with emotion, he read the scroll aloud. When he finished Falcon's story of what had happened, Don looked at Cobra. "It was the vizier who poisoned you, who stole your heart. You can be at peace in the other world now," Don whispered.

He placed the Cobra medallion on the table next to the mummy, then without a look back, he hurried to the vent.

Ali didn't say a word about what he'd just heard, but Don knew that Ali understood.

On the way back to the hotel, they were both silent. The palm trees cast strange shadows, and the streetlights looked like pale, dead moons. They both heard it at the same time and stopped in their tracks.

Sliiip-thud, sliiip-thud, like someone or some thing dragging one foot.

Don looked at Ali, and then they both gave a little laugh. "I'm going to be hearing weird sounds for the rest of my life," Don said.

* * * * *

The next morning as Don was finishing his packing, Ali hammered on his door. "Let me in!" he shouted.

Don opened the door. "What's wrong?"

"Turn on your radio. They're talking about the terrorists."

Don quickly unpacked his radio and switched it to the news.

"*. . . four terrorists confessed to having stored weapons in an empty chamber in the mountain containing the recently discovered tomb of a young prince. The terrorists had been using the chamber long before the discovery of the tomb. Their plans were to try to assassinate the president and take over the country. When archaeologists began excavating the mountain, the terrorists allegedly tried to drive them away using the Mummy's Curse to* *frighten them. They claim the destruction of the tomb was an accident and—this just in—we just received word that the mummy of the young prince disappeared from the museum during the night."*

Don and Ali listened in shocked silence as the news bulletin continued.

"The Director of Antiquities says everything pertaining to the mummy is gone—except for the case it was in and a small urn, the kind used to preserve the heart.

"And it is empty."

About the Author

ALIDA YOUNG and her husband live in the high desert of southern California. She gets many of her ideas by talking with people. She's tried to learn to listen—not just to what people say, but to how they say it. When she's doing a book that requires research, she talks to experts. "Everyone is so helpful," she says. "They go out of their way to help."

Mrs. Young has visited archaeological digs in Egypt, Italy, and Greece. One of her childhood dreams was to be an archaeologist, but she never expected to see the Pyramids or King Tut's tomb. While in Cairo, she stayed at the Tulip Hotel. She walked through the bazaars and the ancient sections of the city. When she travels she likes to get to know the people. "How can you understand what a country's really like," she asks, "if you stay in a tourist hotel and visit only tourist attractions?"

Other books by Alida Young include *Megan the Klutz, Too Young to Die, Never Look Back, Why Am I Too Young?* and *What's Wrong With Daddy?*